Have you ever wondered
who dreamed up Colour?

HUGH'S HUES

written and Illustrated by

COOPER EDENS

Green Tiger Press, Inc.

One particularly gray afternoon Hugh, the only child of the village, set out to deliver pine — nuts to the end of the island.

While he drove his team of horses Hugh looked at the landscape and thought to himself, "Why must everything look the same? Everyday looks just like this!"

in This thought was not new to Hugh; in fact, Hugh was always asking himself this same question. As usual there was no answer, and Hugh became so bored with his surroundings that he feel asleep alongside the road.

This time, however, something happened that would change the world. While Hugh slept he saw the trees and sky and water differently.

The longer he slept the more things
he saw, each with its own different
look. Everything had its special appearance,
and this made Hugh happy.

With all this newness inside him, Hugh got so excited that he woke up.

And though he was back in the old dull world, Hugh was so overwhelmed that he didn't even notice. He quickly turned his coach around and hurried back to tell the villagers what he had seen.

But when Hugh reached town and began his story, he found it difficult to describe what he had no words for. And besides, the villagers were so apathetic that they didn't even try to understand.

From then on, whenever Hugh fell asleep he would see the new look of things, and feel the excitement. He named the pictures he saw "dreams". He called what he felt about them "joy". He tried to get the villagers to pay attention when they slept, but no one listened. For months and months only Hugh experienced the joy of dreams.

As Time went on, Hugh slept more and more, and finally he retired to his hut and slept all the time. At first he slept with a contented smile on his face. Next, the smile turned into a strange grin. Then he began to occasionally chuckle. Finally he laughed out aloud.

Hugh's behaviour drew a most curious crowd to his hut.

The crowd was alarmed by Hugh's laughter, a sound they had never heard. They shook rattles and rang bells over him, but nothing could wake Hugh.

Then the amazing thing happened.

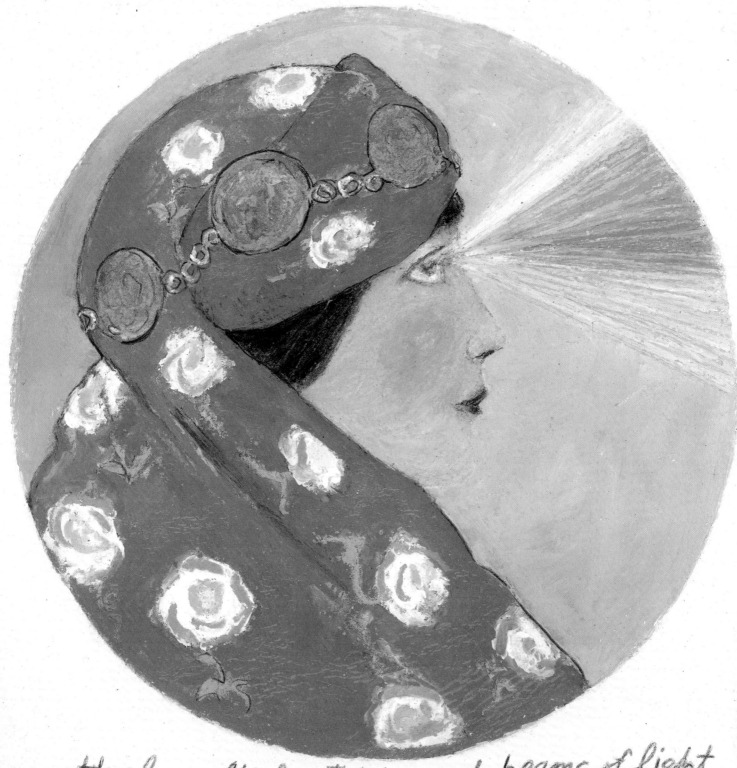

Hugh walked outside and beams of light glowed out of his eyes. The villagers had never seen anything like them, so they called them "Hugh's".

The "Hugh's" horrified everyone in the village, and the leaders immediately called for a meeting.

JAN
THE 1ST
12:00

The leaders ordered that Hugh be placed up in the highest pine-nut tree and that he and his "Hugh's" be ignored.

But no matter found

where the villagers went the

them, and on everyone they stuck.

"Hugh's-

First they threw their huts on top of Hugh, but the "Hugh's" got brighter.

And then they jumped with torches into the "Hugh's", but the "Hugh's" burned even brighter.

Next the leaders poured water on Hugh to cover the "Hugh's" with a lake. The water just vanished? The "Hugh's" were not covered and they were growing.

Next they dug the ground from under Hugh? The ground went down, but the "Hugh's" went on growing. They grew deep into the ground

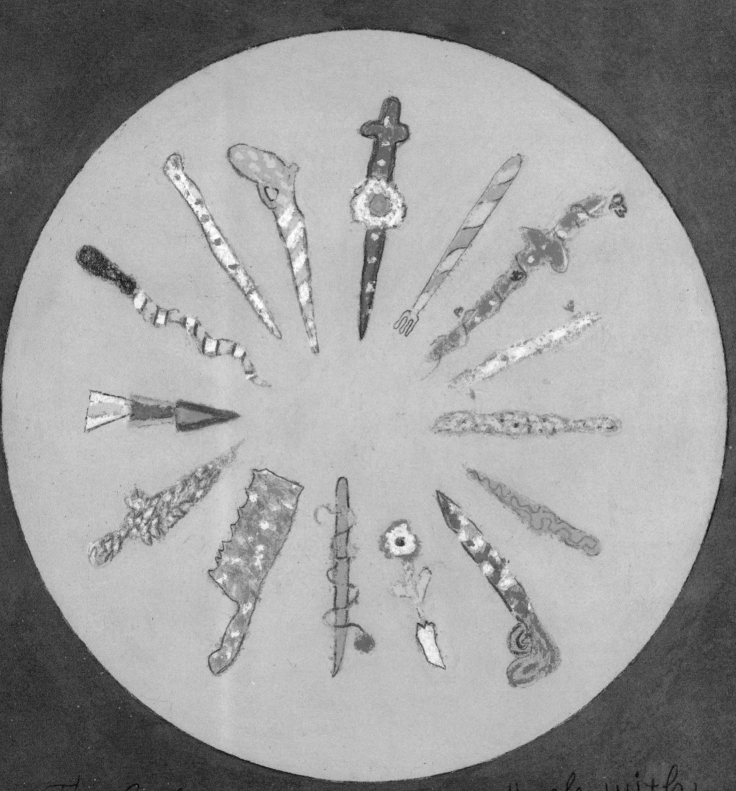

The leaders tried attacking Hugh with weapons, but when the "Hugh's" touched them, they were made harmless.

The leaders tried to beat the "Hugh's" with their fists, but when the "Hugh's" touched them, their fists opened, and they waved peacefully.

The leaders jumped on the "Hugh's", trying to stomp them away, but when they touched them, they began to dance. "Hugh's" got into the eyes of everyone watching and they began to smile.

The dancers began to laugh. Other villagers began to sing. All who saw and heard began themselves to dance and sing.

The villagers who ran away as far as they
could, soon found that the landscape
he "Hugh's" were once inside, was now
inside the "Hugh's". And that
the "Hugh's" had found their way
into everyone's heart.

So what became of Hugh and his "Hugh's"?
Well those ancient leaders, seeing with their
own eyes how much better a colourful world
was to the old gray one, vowed to protect Hugh
and the "Hugh's."

The leaders feared that if Hugh
were ever awakened from his dream of a
colourful world, the world would lose it's
colour.

So to
preserve
Hugh's
sleep the
leaders
put him
in his
coach
and drove
him just beyond
the horizon where
he could dream
undisturbed and
keep the world
colourful.

This is why   when you see
the "Hugh's" beaming up from
the Earth, or bent into an arch
above it, the "Hugh's" are just
beyond the horizon. If you should
attempt to find Hugh himself
the leaders will always drive
his coach a little further
beyond your sight. The ancient
leaders are still devoted to
making sure that Hugh is
not awakened and that
Hugh's Hues continue
to colour the
Earth.